Mr. Smith's Surprising Pet

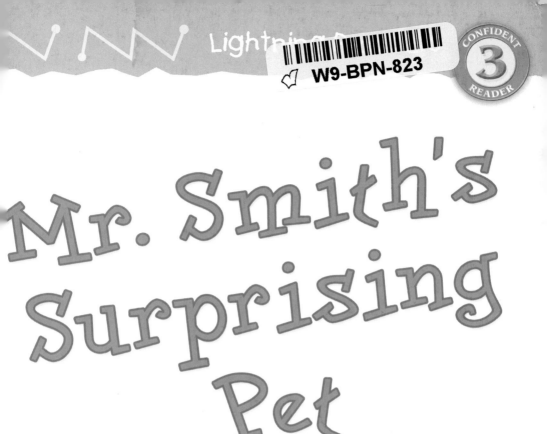

ISBN 0-7696-4021-4

5 0 3 9 5

EAN

9 780769 640211

Library of Congress Cataloging-in-Publication Data

Robinson, Hilary, 1962-
    Mr. Smith's Surprising Per/by Hilary Robinson; illustrated by Tim Archbold.
        p.cm.—(Lightning Readers. Confident Reader 3)
    Includes vocabulary words and discussion questions.
    Summary: The students are skeptical when their teacher claims to own a pet
    dinosaur. Includes vocabulary words and discussion questions.
    ISBN 0-7696-4021-4 (pbk.)
    (1. Pets—Fiction. 2. Teachers—Fiction. 3. Schools—Fiction.) I. Archbold, Tim,
    ill. II.Title. III.Series.

    PZ7.R566175Mr 2005
(E)—dc22   2004060630

School Specialty
Children's Publishing

Text Copyright © Evans Brothers Ltd. 2004. Illustration Copyright © Tim
Archbold 2004. First published by Evans Brothers Limited, 2A Portman Mansions,
Chiltern Street, London W1U 6NR , United Kingdom. This edition published
under license from Zero to Ten Limited. All rights reserved. Printed in China.
This edition published in 2005 by Gingham Dog Press, an imprint of School
Specialty Children's Publishing, a member of the School Specialty Family.

Send all inquires to:
8720 Orion Place
Columbus, OH 43240-2111

ISBN 0-7696-4021-4

2 3 4 5 6 7 8 9 10 EVN 10 09 08 07 06 05

Mr. Smith's Surprising Pet

By Hilary Robinson
Illustrated by Tim Archbold

GINGHAM DOG PRESS

Columbus, Ohio

It was Bring-Your-Pet-to-School Day.
Everyone in Mr. Smith's class was very happy.

The students noticed their teacher
did not have a pet.
"Where is your pet, Mr. Smith?"
asked Andy.

"I left it at home," said Mr. Smith.
"It is too wild to bring to school!"

"Is your pet a bull?" asked Andy.

"Is it an elephant?" asked Julie.

11

"No," said Mr. Smith.
"My pet is a dinosaur."

The students thought Mr. Smith
was joking.
"Have you had it for a very long
time?" asked Andy.

"No," said Mr. Smith.
"I caught it on Saturday.
It eats trees and drinks out
of the bathtub."

"Where did you catch it?" asked Julie.
"I caught it in a dinosaur park,"
replied Mr. Smith.

"I used a large net. I followed the dinosaur tracks."

"Can anyone hunt for a dinosaur?"
asked Andy.

"No," said Mr. Smith.
"You must have a permit.
After you catch one, you get a badge
like mine."

"How do you get a permit?" asked Andy.

"You have to prove that you are a brave dinosaur hunter," said Mr. Smith.

"But you are not brave!" cried the class.

"How do you know that I am not brave?" asked Mr. Smith.

"Because you are scared of little bugs,"
said Andy, holding onto his box.
"In fact, I bet you are scared of..."

"...Max!"

Mr. Smith jumped onto the table.

Maybe he was not so brave after all.

Challenge Words

badge	students
net	wild
permit	

Think About It!

1. Why didn't Mr. Smith bring his pet to school?
2. How did Mr. Smith catch his pet dinosaur?
3. How does someone get a permit to hunt in a dinosaur park?
4. Why didn't the students believe that Mr. Smith was a brave dinosaur hunter?
5. Do you think Mr. Smith really caught a dinosaur? Why or why not?
6. Which part of the story do you think could be real? Which part is pretend?

The Story and You

1. If you could have a dinosaur for a pet, would you want one?
2. How do you think you would take care of a pet dinosaur?
3. If you could have any pet you wanted, what kind of animal would you choose?
4. Describe a time when you were very brave.